U0033237

你好，我在找一位我深愛的女友
臭B，她走失了，請告訴她，我很愛她

MISSING PERSON NOTIC:
I AM LOOKING FOR MY BELOVED gf,
SHE HAS GONE FAR, IF YOU SEE HER
PLS LET ME KNOW

在自己的小宇宙裏 用眼睛

看見世界真實的樣子

0932-453545

人生，總會遇到想找回生命中最愛的人的時候

現代絕版痴情男 aHsien 著

我回來了，妳卻從我心出國了但我相信

妳知道我是最疼妳的．

就讓過去隨風飄．

我再重新追求妳．可以嗎！是.B

I HAVE RETURNED BUT YOU HAVE LEFT MY HEART

I BELIEVE THAT YOU KNOW FOR SURE THAT YOU

ARE WHAT I CHERISH THE MOST.

LET THE WIND BLOW AWAY THE PAST, I AM

GOING TO START CHASING YOU AGAIN.

Dayl

送給郎～

← 限時掛號
直達她ˊ♥心。

畫圖最快樂

THE HAPPIEST TIME
IS WHEN I AM DRAWING!

Day2

的花束，獻給妳
THIS IS THE VERY FIRST
TIME I SEND YOU FLOWERS.
THANKS FOR ALWAYS
FORGIVING ME.

哼

Day3

拔拔會很乖 不敢再惹妳生氣了

I'LL BE BB's GOOD BOY WILL NOT MAKE YOU ANGRY EVER AGAIN.

NO KIDDING. No KIDDING

Day4

拔拔會像小天使般的照顧妳，
妳要細心品味～。

IF YOU LOOK CAREFULLY YOU'LL SEE THAT I'D LIKE TO BE YOUR ANGEL!

Day5

臭B，挨挨的潛力好還沒有完全發掘！

MY LOVE,

GOTTA DIG HARDER, HARDER, HARDER.... I HAVE LOTS OF POTENTIAL ONLY YOU CAN DISCOVER!!

Day6

Day7

即,再給它一次機會,
也給按按一次機會

GIVE "him" A CHANCE
AND GIVE "MOi" A
CHANCE TOO!

Day8

我覺得我可以
讓妳依賴。

I'M NOT
SHITTING

TRULY YOU CAN
ALWAYS RELY ON ME!

Day9

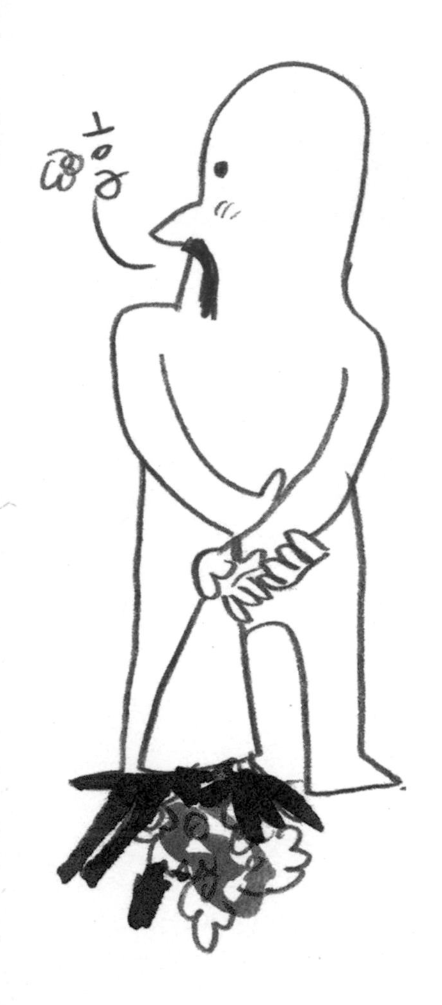

我想妳最好要把
这些卡片收好，免
得以後無法發大財！

I SUGGEST YOU, KEEP THESE
DOODLES otherwise
YOU WILL CRY FOR
LOSING TONS OF MONEY.

Day10

BB, "LOVE" IS JUST LIKE A SWITCH.
I WILL WAIT FOR YOU
TO TURN IT BACK ON AGAIN

BB，愛就像是個開關。
我等妳重新打開

Day11

Hey BB, WHAT CHA DOING?
THINKING OF ME?!

妳說"沒有感覺"了
"沒有感覺"到底
是什麼感覺!?

Day12

不管我怎麼忙
就是想到妳，怎麼辦？

BB. NO MATTER HOW BUSY I AM
I STILL THINKING OF YOU

Day13

我好想跟妳說，我好想
好想跟妳在公園分享我
的喜怒哀樂！

BB, I SO WANTED TO SIT IN
THE PARK WITH YOU SHARING
MY HAPPY, ANGRY, SAD AND joyful THINGS

臭B.如果還有机會,拔拔
想帶妳去美國、日本.義大利
…對啦,還有西藏!!

EVEN WITH ITS BITSY
CHANCE I'D STILL LIKE TO
TAKE YOU TO SF, JAPAN,
ITALY.... Oh,, and TIBET!

Day15

Oh STOP YOU TWO,
STOP KISSING!!!

哦~No.
別再親了.
你們倆位
~.

Day16

常常在想，
不知道會不會跟妳在街上不期而遇.

CONSTANTLY THINKING
"WOULD I MEET YOU ON THE STREET BY COINCIDENCE?!"

我不喜歡週休二日，因為這兩天
妳都不在家，也不接我電話。

I DON'T LIKE WEEKEND OFF
BECAUSE THOSE DAYS
YOU DON'T PICK UP MY CALL !!

Day18

I WOULD LIKE No.4, THANKS

這是我們分開後，我第一次去
肯德基，點了我們最愛的"四號"餐

BB, I AM INDEED A BIG "33 YEAR OLD" KID.

對，我真的像小孩子，

我是**33**歲的老孩子。

Day20

每到週末
我還是不自主
的想問妳.
要喝溫咖啡
對不對?

BB, WHEN IT COMES
TO THE WEEKEND I STILL
CAN'T STOP BUT TO ASK YOU,
"WOULD YOU LIKE
HOT OR WARM COFFEE?"

對不起，昨天又惹妳生氣了！不要再生氣了好嗎!?

SORRY BB I HAVE MADE YOU MAD AGAIN?
CAN YOU NOT BE MAD AT ME??

Day22

我有好多話好想跟妳說
但我不敢⋯⋯

BB, I HAVE SO MANY THINGS TO
SHARE WITH BUT I AM AFRAID..

Day23

影子啊！我想你也跟我一樣
"孤單"吧！

SHADOW, I THINK YOU ARE AS
LONELY AS I AM.

Day24

新家的大沙發是我另一個避難所

THE SOFA IN THE NEW HOUSE is
MY OTHER HIDING PLACE.

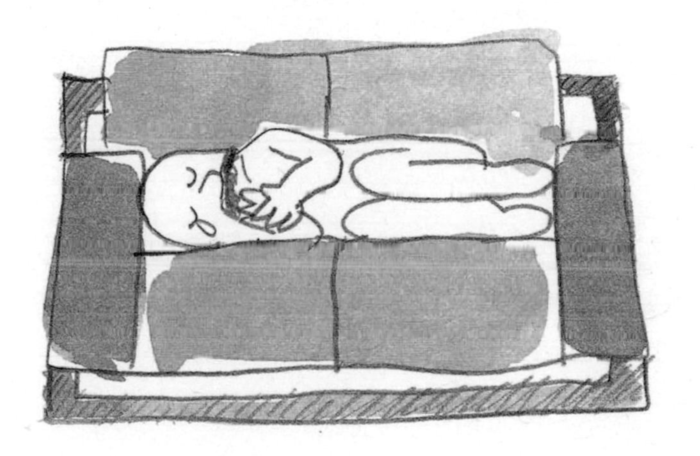

Day25

我終於知道
晚上發冷的原因了！
那是因為少了妳～～

I KNOW WHY I FEEL SO
COLD AT NIGHT, THAT IS
WITHOUT U!!

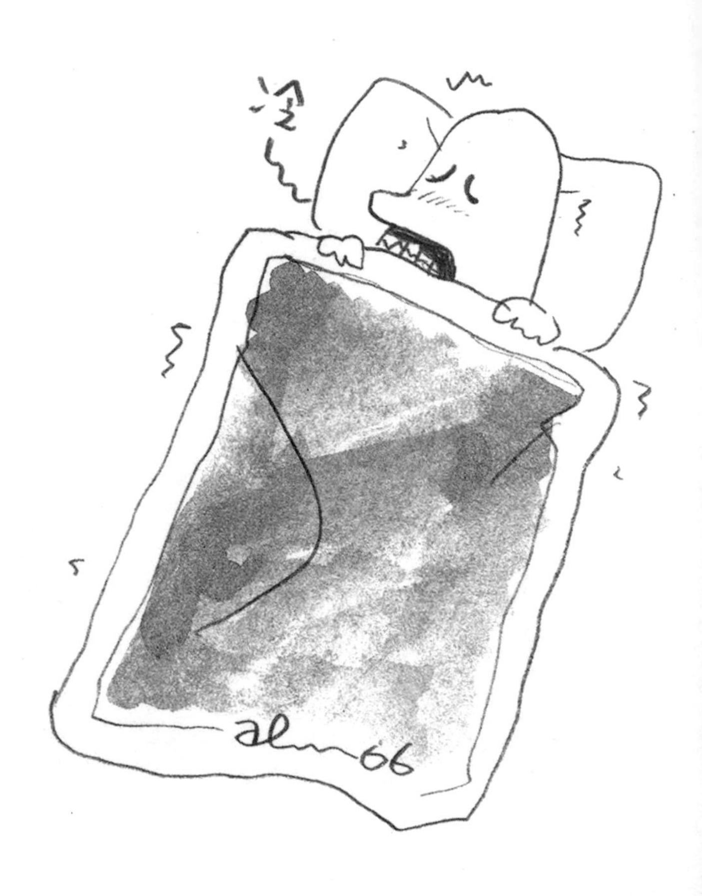

Day26

MY HEART IS EMPTY MAKES
ME FEEL COLD NO MATTER
HOW MANY CLOTHES I HAVE PUT ON.

Day27

為什麼今年春天這麼多雨，
煩死了!!

HOW COME THIS YEAR HAS
SO MANY RAINING DAYS !?

Day28

臭B啊！記不記得"剪刀腳"
每次看电視，我們都會堆疊双腿～

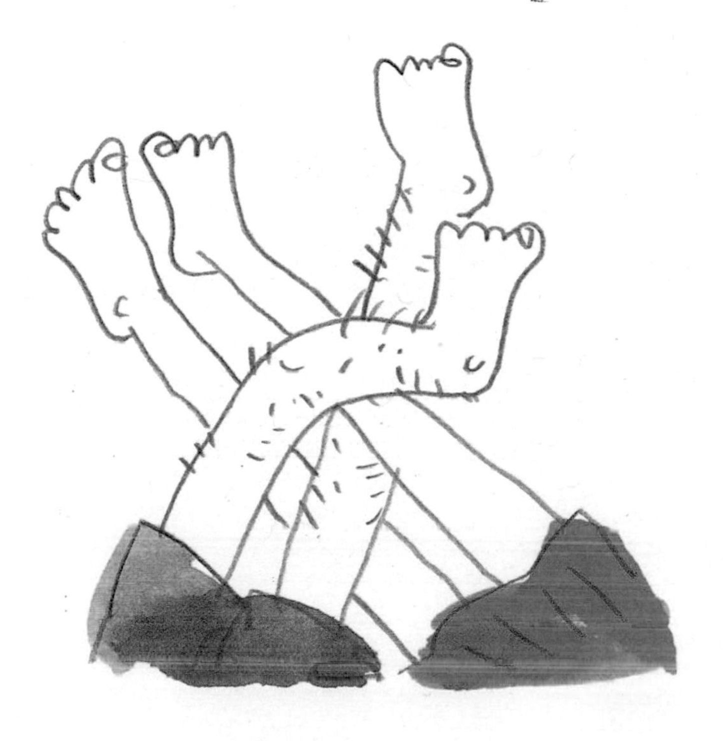

BB DO YOU REMEMBER OUR SWEET HOUR OF "SCISSOR FEET" INFRONT OF THE TV?

不好意思今天腦袋一陣空，
哇哇哇．畫不出來啊～．

BB, SORRIE TODAY MY BRAIN
WENT BLANK CANNOT ~~DRAWING~~
DRAW ANYTHING...

Day30

好吧，妳說要慢慢來，
我就"慢慢來"

OKAY, YOU SAID TAKE IT SLOW THEN
I WILL SLOW LIKE A SNAIL.

Day31

這些是我在美國時幫妳保留，
要等妳來找我時給妳用的...現在，
我把它們帶回臺灣了！

THESE ARE THE ONES I BOUGHT IN US
FOR YOU TO USE WHEN YOU COME VISIT.
BUT I HAVE BROUGHT THEM
BACK TO TAIWAN NOW.

Day32

BB, YOU SAID YOU HAD NIGHTMARES OF US BREAKING UP NOW THE NIGHTMARE HAVE COME TRUE. SNIFF, SNIFF...

貝B，妳常說妳作惡夢，
夢到我們會分開；
但這次這個
惡夢成真了

分手時，"親朋好友"有存在
的必要，真的有用。

AT HEARTBROKEN TIMES
FAMILIES AND FRIENDS
ARE GOOD TO HAVE AROUND!

Day34

快快快，先將重要聯絡人填好
免得到時後找無人訴苦....

Name: ______________________ Ph: ______________
Email: ______________________________________

Name: ______________________ Ph: ______________
Email: ______________________________________

Name: ______________________ Ph: ______________
Email: ______________________________________

Name: ______________________ Ph: ______________
Email: ______________________________________

Name: ______________________ Ph: ______________
Email: ______________________________________

Name: ______________________ Ph: ______________
Email: ______________________________________

Name: ______________________ Ph: ______________
Email: ______________________________________

Name: ______________________ Ph: ______________
Email: ______________________________________

Name: ______________________ Ph: ______________
Email: ______________________________________

Name: ______________________ Ph: ______________
Email: ______________________________________

Name: ______________________ Ph: ______________
Email: ______________________________________

突然間，我才明瞭我已不再是妳依賴的那位拔拔，而是一位永不曝光的密友，但我會加油，請妳用心看！

NOW. I KNOW I AM NOT THE PERSON YOU SHARE UR HEART TO BUT I WILL LET U SEE MY CHANGE

Day36

臭蒼蠅走開，跟她是我
這隻蒼蠅王的。

SMELLY FLIES : I WARN YOU
BRANDY IS MINE SO GET OUT!!

Day37

郎，挨挨還是會等到哪天
這個電話再傳來妳的聲音！
Hey U, HOW LONG DO I HAVE TO
WAIT FOR U TO RING
ME AGAIN?

Day38

不管前面的路如何走?!

有"我"好嗎?

BB NO MATTER WHAT YOUR ROAD IS FOR THE FUTURE PLS INCLUDE ME WITH YOU !!

Day39

放心，一切有我罩B!
DON'T WORRY, U STILL
GOT ME RIGHT HERE!

Day40

寶B,
沒什大不了的，天塌下來我可挺著啦。

BB,
NOTHING BIG DEAL!
INDEED.

Day41

寶B.睡吧 好好的睡.我會一直
守衛到妳醒過來。

SLEEP TIGHT MY SWEETIE. ILL BE
HERE PROTECTING YOU TILL YOU WAKE UP.

Day42

JUST GIVE ME A RING

0930-X2XX3X

工商服務

Day43

貝B，把心再還給
揍揍 好不好!?

BB, COULD YOU PLS GIVE
ME BACK MY HEART?!
PLS....

Day45

臭B，沒有妳的人生
是缺一半的，我真的愛妳

OH, B WITHOUT YOU,
"LIFE" IS JUST HALF AND EMPTY.
I REALLY LOVE YOU.

Day46

BB 今天风雨交加，妳自己多注意安全唷

BB,
toDAY is THUNDERY AND WINDY DAY SO BE CAREFUL OUT THERE OKAY?

BB.我想是我不夠好，才留不住妳；
但其實我一直在做改變．
我好想好想妳

BB, I THINK I AM NOT GOOD ENOUGH
OTHERWISE YOU WOULDN'T LEAVE.
BUT..BUT... I AM CHANGING BIT BY BIT,
CAN YOU SEE?

Day48

妳還是住在我心中哦,
水、電、瓦斯、第四台全免。

BB YOU STILL ARE AND
ALWAYS IN MY HEART.
LOVE YA!

Day49

臭B，技甚累了，早點睡吧~..

BB. I AM TIRED GOING TO BED NOW.

Day50

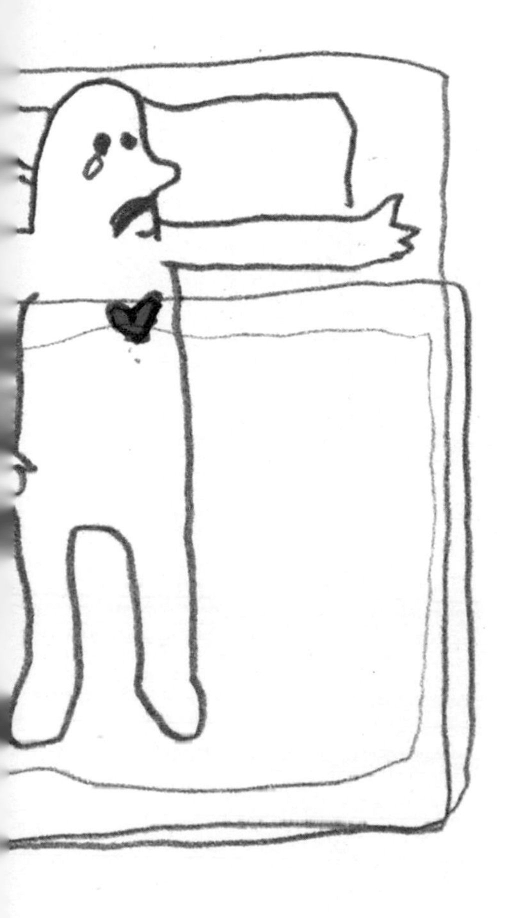

還是習慣將床
留一大塊給妳.

I STILL HAVE HOPE. I'LL WAIT
TILL THE DAY YOU COME BACK.

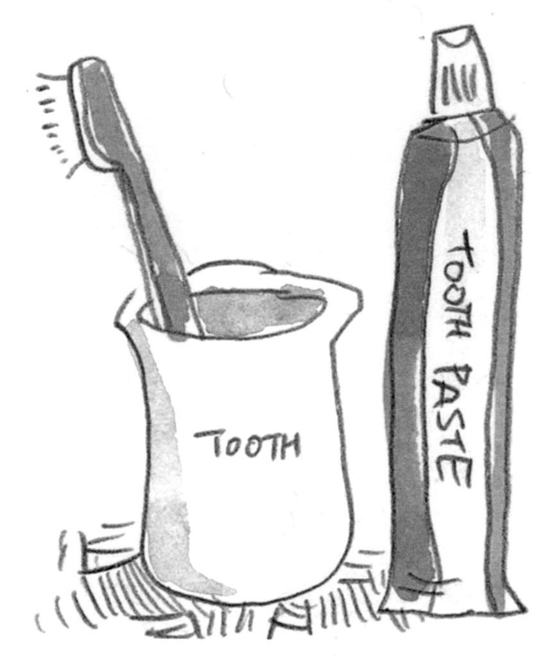

是B啊!!
妳的新牙刷
還在等妳哦~.

BB, UR NEW BRUSH is
STILL WAITING FOR YOU

Day52

我今天又去那家餃子店了
老闆娘又問說"妳怎麼沒跟我來"?

BB, TODAY I WENT TO THE DUMPLING
RESTAURANT AGAIN AND THE LADY OWER
ASK ME HOW COME U DIDN'T COME WITH ME!?

BB.記不記得拔拔說過我們最好有兩台電視,我昨晚認真想過,如果有兩台電視,我們要放哪?

BB. REMEMBER WE SAID THAT WE ~~would~~ SHOULD
HAVE 2 TVs? LAST NIGHT I SERIOUSLY THINK
IT OVER AND OVER!
WELL... WHERE SHALL WE PUT OUR 2 TVs?

Day54

臭B，我會把"信任"存滿，

拿送給妳，迎回妳

BB, I WILL REBUILD THE "TRUST"

WAITING FOR YOU TO RETURN

BB, DO YOU REMEMBER THIS JOKE?
IT'S OUR CLASSIC
你什麼意思!!
我我我……
不好意思。

從沒看過像我神經
這麼大條的男朋友!!

NEVER SEEN A
DUMMER BOYFRIEND
THAN ME.

Day57

分手時的處方簽1.2.3

INGREDIENT FOR BREAKUPS:

#1 CHATTING WITH BB (DOSAGE 30MIN)

#2 MEET BB FACE 2 FACE (DOSAGE 2 HOURS)

#3 TWO HEART BIDING CLOSELY TOGETHER (DOSAGE FOREVER)

② 跟臭B見一面
幸效 2小時

兩顆心
③ 緊緊相靠!
幸效永遠

Day59

別管朋友結婚去，我只要我們繼續牽手走下去!

NO MATTER HOW LONG I WILL WAIT. RIGHT NOW I JUST WANT TO HOLD YOU TIGHT FOREVE AND EVER.

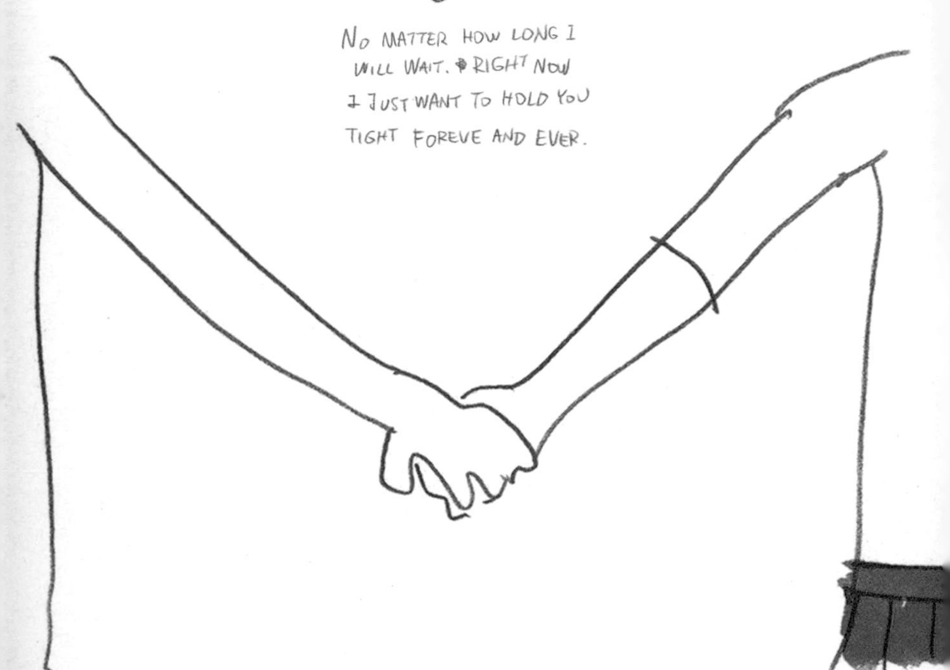

Day60

我喜歡被妳帶著走
的感覺，真的很愛

BB, I LOVE THE FEELING OF U LEADING ME
VERY VERY VERY MUCH

Day61

如果这個分開，是可以讓
我們的未來幸福美滿！我願意

BB, IF THIS BREAKUP IS FOR US TO
BECOME MORE HAPPIER, THEN I OBEY

Day62

貝.B 妳的心，拔拔先幫妳保管.
直到妳回來。

BB. LET ME KEEP YOUR HEART
WITH ME UNTIL YOU RETURN.

Day63

"阿嬤"像太陽一樣
溫暖妳我的心.

A-MA IS JUST LIKE SUNSHINE
WARMING UP OUR HEARTS.

Day64

HEY! DID YOU FORGET TO PAY
YOUR CELL PHONE BILL AGAIN?

Day65

不管要花多大的力氣，
我都要把妳追回來！

NO MATTER OF HOW MUCH
EFFORT.... I WILL CHASE YOU BACK.

Day66

不管要花多久的時間，
我都要把妳等回來.

BB. NO MATTER HOW LONG
I'LL WAIT HERE TILL YOU
GET BACK.

Day67

我的心留了個大位給妳，因為我
好愛好愛妳

BB, I SAVE A BIG SPOT FOR YOU IN MY
HEART CAUSE I LOVE U SO SO SO MUCH

Day68

Day69

貝.B 讓按接把我們的結打開！

BB, LET ME UNTIE OUR HEART'S KNOT

Day70

趕快提筆 記下你跟他(她)的甜蜜點滴，可別像我 後悔莫及呀

大傘包小傘，

我習慣幫妳遮風、擋雨

HONEY, I STILL LIKE TO

TAKE CARE OF EVERYTHING

FOR YOU!

不知道妳的心發生了
什麼事!? 但我很想
試著了解

I DONNO WHAT HAPPEN
TO OUR LOVE BUT I REALLY
DO TRY TO KNOW.

Day73

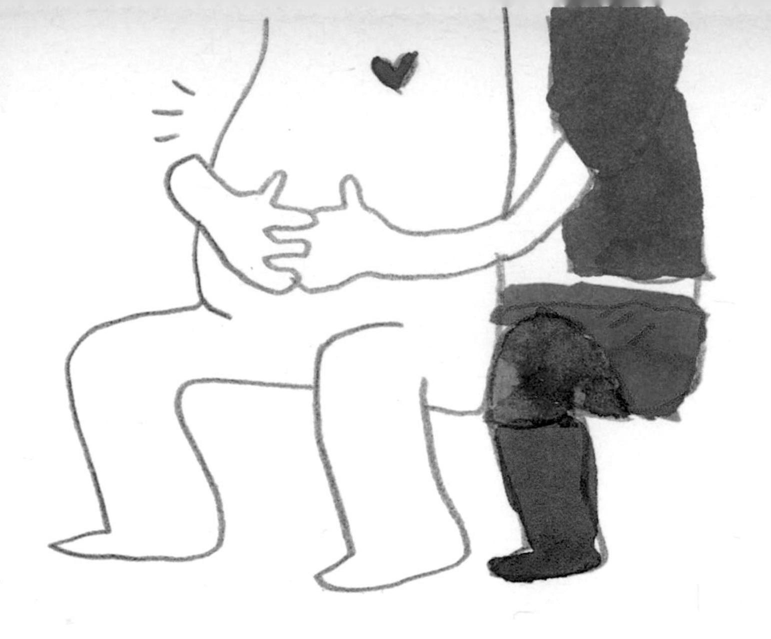

臭B，拔拔喜歡妳扣上"安全帶"的感覺

BB, I LIKE THE FEELING
YOU HOLD ME.

Day74

BB，我們是“城市双煞”

人見人怕

BB, WE ARE CITY'S FEARFUL COUPLE!

"SEE US FEAR US"

0518 2006.
外婆 BYE BYE。

05/18/2006.
Good Bye
My Dearest Grand Ma.

Day76

假如有世界末日那一天，
我希望我手牽的還是妳

BB, I LOVE TO HOLD YOUR HAND TILL.
THE END OF THE WORLD

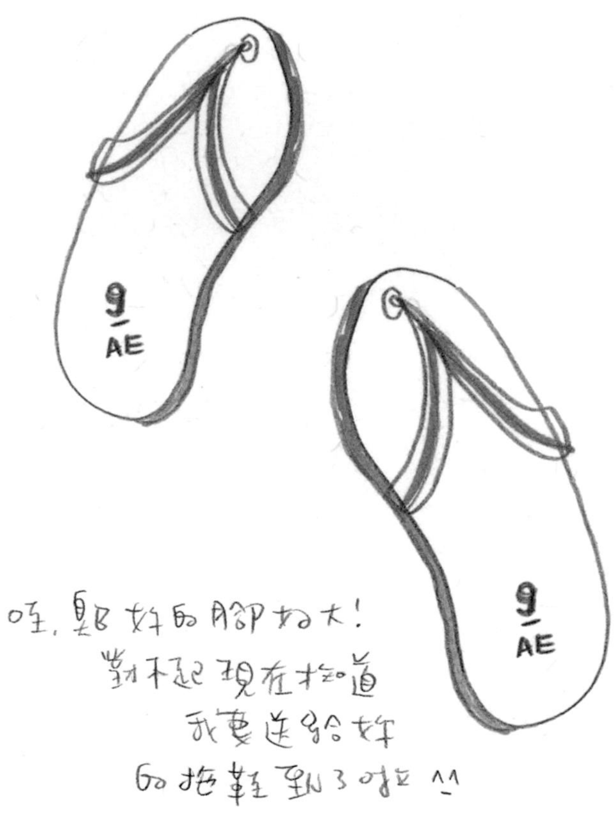
9
AE
9
AE
哇，BB妳的腳好大！
對不起現在才知道
我要送給妳
的拖鞋到了啦 ^^
WOW, BB I DIDN'T KNOW YOU HAVE A BIG FEET!
THE FLIP THAT I BOUGHT FOR YOU HAS ARRIVED

Day78

拔拔偷偷告訴妳，我買了兩個巫毒娃娃
效用是"復合"。分手也會使人呆，哈哈哈……

BB TELL YOU A SECRET I HAVE BOUGHT
TWO VOODOO DOLLARS FOR THE PURPOSE
OF GETTING BACK TOGETHER!

BB.如果妳願意，妳還是可以
"狡兔三窟"

BB. YOU CAN STAY AT MY HOME
ANYTIME YOU WISH

Day80

Day81

BB 拔拔好想跟妳去吃燒肉哦!

BB, I SO WANT TO
HAVE BBQ WITH YOU O!

Day82

今天

WINSON幫我剪一個"帥"到不行
的髮型啊~

BB, TODAY WINSON CUT ME
A SUPERB
HANDSOME HAIR

人家說，溝通就像是在挖通隧道。
那，拔拔會努力挖，不管需要多久

PEOPLE SAID COMMUNICATION IS JUST
LIKE A TUNNEL. AND I'LL KEEP
DIGGING DIGGING AND DIGGING

還是很想念被妳"牽扯"的感覺

BB, I MISS THE TIMES WHEN YOU TIDE ME
WITH YOUR LOVE

Day86

臭B，拔拔住的這裏可以看到101喔.
這樣跨年就不需要人擠人了！

Sweetie, I CAN SEE 101 FROM MY PLACE
,SO NEW YEAR COUNT DOWN WE
DON'T HAVE "PEOPLE
PUSH PEOPLE' La...

Day87

來吧！讓我變成"邱比特"吧！
COME, LET ME BECOME CUPID!

Day88

BB，只要我有心跳，我就會默默的愛妳關心妳，奮戰努力到最後。我真的愛妳

BB, I'LL FIGHT FOR U TILL THE DAY I DIE. I DO LOVE U WITH MY LIFE, it's TRUE

時間到！限時於今晚子夜前回到我身邊

"逾時不候"

TIMES UP!

COME BACK BEFORE MID-NIGHT
OTHERWISE NO MORE WAITING!!
(JUST KIDDING la!)

復合問卷調查表

親愛的，妳考慮一下，跟我在一起好不！

（請在認為對的事情打☑）

1. □ 兩人在一起睡，我會幫妳暖被，因為我都比妳早睡。

2. □ 兩人去吃大餐才有感覺也才不會吃不完浪費。

3. □ 有我在，我可以幫妳處理掉所有3C產品的問題

4. □ 有妳在，我就可以在妳面前撒嬌，逗妳笑。還有捏妳的小鳥嘴。

5. □ 我們在一起是最速配的，因為老天爺眼紅要拆散我們。

以上五項都打☑

那我們就可以又在一起了！

已經第100天了吔！
妳還會記得我的好嗎!?

It's ALREADY THE 100th day, Do YOU
STILL REMEMBER MY GOODNESS?

Day92

妳的最愛是小叮噹
我的最愛是妳
BEAUTIFUL YOU, NERVOUS ME.

Day93

Day94

妳很棒，妳真的很棒，真的
好啦，我們都很棒！

U ARE GOOD. U ARE GREAT,
U ARE FANTASTIC, IT'S TRUE LA.
OK. WE ARE ALL FATASTICALLY GOOD

皂.B.以前妳是拔拔的頭號粉絲
，現在我是妳的後援會會長

BB IN THE PAST YOU ARE MY #1 FAN.
NOW I HAVE BECOME THE BB FAN
CLUB'S CHAIRMAN!

Day96

BB，不管它是什麼，我都願意幫妳分擔。

BB, I DONNO ~~WHAT~~ IT'S GOOD OR BAD, BUT LET ME SHARE IT WITH YOU

BB's 壓力

OH yeah, MAY I STILL ASK YOU OUT
TO SHOPPING AND MOVie?

對了.明天我可以
約妳去信義誠品
看電影唷!?

害羞

Day99

哇,鼠B,我被妳拒絕的次數竟有

15 次之多

WOW. YOU HAVE REJECTED MORE 15
TIME ALREADY AND STILL COUNTING...

BB妳知道嗎?
妳不笑的時候,
好兇好兇好兇.

BB, DO YOU KNOW
WHEN YOU ARE NOT SMILLING
YOU LOOK SO MEAN, VERY MEAN

我會跟 保誠人壽一樣
"用心傾聽妳的聲音"

BEING UR GOOD LISTENER is MY #1 JOB.

Day103

① 你和他(她)六個
最值得紀念的日子與記憶

	WHEN:	WHERE:	WHAT:
1.			
2.			
3.			
4.			
5.			
6.			

BB. 我把對妳的思念都在
畫中的妳跟妳說了, 但我好想
抱抱真的妳.

BB, I PUT ALL OF MY FOR YOU IN
MY DRAWING BUT I WOULD ALL
THESE JUST TO HOLD YOU IN PERSON

我的心慢慢"回溫"了

HA, MY HEART is SLIGHTLY WARMER NOW.

我收到妳傳給我的留言。
高興的快哭了

YOU SENT ME A TEXT MESSAGE !!

I BURST OUT JOYFUL TEARS..

Day107

看来我是有打動妳的心了!!

MMM... LOOKS LIKE I HAVE
TOUCHED YOUR HEART

Day108

SNIFF... SNIFF.., I AM SO TOUCHED.
YOU SAID "LET'S GO MOVIE SATURDAY."

呼呼呼…分手後第一次碰面，
到底該穿啥好呢？

HUM... HUM... WHAT SHOULD I WEAR TO SEE BB? NERVOUS...

Day110

後會有期了！親朋、好友、網友、借我錢
與欠我錢的人再見，BYE BYE

Good BYE FAMILIES, BUDDIES, ONLINE FRIENDS,
LENDERS AND BORROWERS, GOOD BYE

Day111

HOOYA, We have got together~~

Day112

後記

從沒想過
自己能有一本書。要感謝的人
實在太多，謝謝大家購
買它。謝謝離開我身邊
又回來的臭B，謝謝親愛
的朋友們，謝謝"自轉"
社長！謝謝把我養成
這樣的老爸老媽…還有我
妹妹．一堆人…謝謝x500

aHsien 2006/06

Beautiful Day 04

0932-453545

·作者／aHsien
·編輯／黃俊隆
·編輯創意／陳宜伶
·企劃／黃俊隆
·美術設計／aHsien ·英文修訂／Jean Tseng
·出版者／自轉星球文化創意事業有限公司
·住址／台北市106大安區和平東路三段308巷15弄37號1樓
·電子信箱／hesaid.hesaid@msa.hinet.net
·電話／(02)8732-1629 ·傳真／(02)8732-1629
·總經銷／創智文化有限公司
·住址／台北縣235中和市建一路136號5樓
·電話／(02)2228-9828
·印刷／永暘彩色印刷有限公司
·住址／台北市西園路二段281巷6弄30號4樓
·電話／(02)2309-3232

國家圖書館出版品預行編目資料

《0932-453545》aHsien 文.圖 -- 初版
台北市：自轉星球文化，2006［民95］
面；公分
ISBN 957-28747-4-8（平裝）
855 95011342

PRINTED IN TAIWAN

2006年07月初版
定價：新台幣220元

ISBN 957-28747-4-8

堅持每年四本的好味道